**Kirklees**
COUNCIL

Lib
Re
Huc
HD2

This book should be returned on or before tl
Fines are charged if the item is late.

You may renew this loan for a further period by phone, personal visit or at
www.kirklees.gov.uk/libraries, provided that the book is not required by
another reader.

NO MORE THAN THREE RENEWALS ARE PERMITTED

Bloomsbury Education
An imprint of Bloomsbury Publishing Plc

50 Bedford Square
London
WC1B 3DP
UK

1385 Broadway
New York
NY 10018
USA

www.bloomsbury.com

BLOOMSBURY and the Diana logo are trademarks of Bloomsbury Publishing Plc

First published in 2010 by A & C Black, an imprint of Bloomsbury Publishing Plc

A catalogue record for this book is available from the British Library.

ISBN
PB: 978 1 4729 4213 5
epub: 978 1 4729 5232 5
epdf: 978 1 4729 5231 8

2 4 6 8 10 9 7 5 3 1

Typeset by Newgen Knowledge Works (P) Ltd., Chennai, India

Printed and bound in UK by CPI Group (UK) ltd, Croydon CR0 4YY

MIX
Paper from
responsible sources
FSC® C020471

This book is produced using paper that is made from wood grown in managed, sustainable forests.
It is natural, renewable and recyclable. The logging and manufacturing processes conform to the
environmental regulations of the country of origin.

To find out more about our authors and books visit www.bloomsbury.com. Here you will find extracts,
author interviews, details of forthcoming events and the option to sign up for our newsletters.

TERRY DEARY

VIKING TALES

THE EYE OF THE VIKING GOD

Inside illustrations by Helen Flook

BLOOMSBURY EDUCATION
AN IMPRINT OF BLOOMSBURY

LONDON   OXFORD   NEW YORK   NEW DELHI   SYDNEY

CHAPTER ONE
FLEECE

Norway, 793

The girl had no name. She had been snatched from her family when she was a small child and had never known what her father and mother had called her.

She had been taken by the Viking raiders to be a slave back on their ice-blown, grey-grassed, mud-pathed, stony-field village across the sea. They had thrown her in the bottom of their longboat. She was too shocked to cry. If she died on the cold sea journey, she died, the Vikings said.

But the girl lived and was kept as a slave by one of the raiders, a Viking farmer.

The farmer let her eat scraps from his table. He made her feed the chickens and gather firewood. She slept in the loft of his barn with the warmth of the cows below to keep her warm.

The farmer's family hardly ever spoke to her. Sometimes the small, round-faced, spiteful son shouted at her.

"Fetch me some bread and cheese. Understand, English slave? Bread. Cheese. Fast. Or I beat you with my stick."

His name was Sigurd, and he was about her age.

When the girl grew older, she was sent out into the bleak boulders of the hills to look after the sheep and lambs. She built herself a small hut from rocks for shelter. It was high on the hill, and looked down on the village below and over the sea towards England and the home she had forgotten.

When an old sheep died, the girl skinned it with a sharp stone and made herself a coat to keep out the winter winds. She wore it with the wool on the inside and was the only person in the village to have such a coat. They called her 'Fleece-girl' and then 'Fleece'. Now the girl had a name. Of sorts.

In the summer, the warriors sailed away in three longboats the villagers had built. Before the autumn gales arrived, they returned with stolen corn, cows and sheep. Sometimes they had golden crosses and silver cups, which they'd taken from the monks, they said.

That last autumn they had returned with barrels of honey-wine the English monks had made.

Sigurd had sneered at the girl. "We are having a great feast in the hall tonight. I'll be there. We'll roast a whole ox and drink the English honey-wine. If you are good, I may save you a bone to chew on. Would you like that, Fleece?"

"Yes, Master Sigurd," she said quietly. If she didn't call him 'master' he would kick her until she ached.

"Now go and gather wood from the hills. We'll be having a huge fire to roast that ox. I will eat and eat until my belly is stuffed," he smirked.

Fleece turned and went to fetch a sledge. She would load it high with broken branches and drag it over the rocky paths back to the village.

Some warriors wandered through the village and she had to step aside to let them pass. If she didn't, they'd slap her with their swords. It would hurt her more than Sigurd with his soft-booted feet. They were huge men with arms thicker than any branch she could lift. Their beards were ragged and matted, and their bodies smelled of stale sweat and fish. Their eyes were colder than the North Sea.

Fleece ran to the hills.

CHAPTER TWO
ODIN'S EYE

That night, Fleece was told to serve at the feast.

"I'll be watching you," Sigurd hissed, as she passed his table. "Take one crumb from the plates you're serving and I'll have you thrown into the sea."

The girl gave a single nod and carried on running from the tables to where the cooks were carving the meat.

The ox was on a pole over the fire. It took two boys to turn the animal as it sizzled and dropped oozing fat into the fire pit below. Slaves waited with wooden plates ready to be filled with food.

As Fleece hurried to serve Sigurd, a huge hand reached out to grab her wrist. "I'll have that plate, slave," the man said.

His fair hair and beard were as greasy as the ox and his pale eyes sparkled in the light of the flickering torches. It was Askold, the warrior chief. Fleece passed him the plate. He tore at a piece of meat with one hand and held a drinking cup in the other.

Fleece hurried back to the fire to take a new plate to Sigurd. The boy passed her a rib bone. "There you are, slave girl," he said. "There is your payment." The boy's eyes were as damp as the stream that ran through the river. He had been supping at the honey-wine and it was dribbling from the corner of his mouth.

Fleece tucked the rib bone into a small pocket she had made in her coat. There was a great crash from the table behind her. Askold had slammed his sword onto the table and risen to his feet. The other Vikings fell quiet.

"A tale," the warrior chief demanded. "Let the poet begin!" He sat down heavily, spilling his cup of wine.

A thin old man walked slowly to the end of the hall as the Vikings cheered. He stood on a small platform and looked around. "What is it to be?" he asked.

"Odin!" someone cried out, and the crowd cheered.

Fleece sat on the earth floor by the platform. No one would be eating while the poet told his tale... which was Fleece's favourite.

The poet began to chant the story of the great Viking god Odin.

"And the god he came to the Wisdom Well
That stood in the land of the giants.

He was dressed like a traveller, in cloak of blue,
And in his hand a wooden staff.

A giant stood guard at the Wisdom Well
He would not let great Odin drink
Unless he gave a single eye
And let it fall in the water deep."

Fleece was warmed by the fire, but she shuddered because she knew what came next.

Odin let the giant pluck out an eye and then he drank the magical water. As he drank, the god saw the past, the present and the future. He saw all the sorrows and troubles that would fall upon both men and gods.

When the tale was ended, Askold rose to his feet and held his wine cup out to be filled. Slaves hurried around the hall to fill the cups. Fleece carried a jug to Sigurd, but the boy had already fallen asleep.

"Praise to the great god Odin," Askold cried, "who gave his eye so he could drink from the well of wisdom and make sure the

Vikings would rule the world!"

The Vikings cheered until the reed roof shook. They drank until all the barrels were running dry and one by one they fell asleep in the smoky air.

CHAPTER THREE
THE TRAVELLER

The cockerel crowed next morning. Fleece jumped up from the straw and hurried down the ladder. She gathered a handful of corn and fed the chickens. Then she collected the eggs. There were more than usual this morning. She cracked one and

swallowed it whole. Fleece clutched the rib bone in her pocket. She would have that as a special treat when she'd done her morning's work. Her mouth became wet at the smell and thought of eating meat. She placed the rest of the eggs in a basket inside the empty farmhouse.

The village was quiet. No smoke rose from the chimneys and no women rushed to milk the cows. Even the dogs were silent, feeling fat and sleepy with the bones from the feast.

The girl hurried past the hall and heard the sound of snoring. Someone coughed, and another man groaned. They would sleep until the sun was high in the sky.

Fleece crossed the bridge over the stream and headed up the hill to a clump of trees too small to be called a wood. As she turned onto the path to gather wood, she saw a leather sheet stretched between two small trees.

A man sat on the ground, striking flints to make a fire. He wore a large hat with a wide brim that shaded his face. "Good morning," he said in a strange voice.

Fleece knew he wasn't from this part of the world. "Good morning," she said quietly.

"You're out early," the man said.

"I'm gathering wood so the farmer and his family will have a fire when they get back from the hall. They're still sleeping after the feast last night."

The stranger gave a sigh. "I once went to feasts. I loved roast ox. Now I live on any berries and nuts I can find in the forest. You don't have any roast meat, do you?"

Fleece clutched her rib bone. "I... I... I'm

just a slave."

"I wouldn't ask," the stranger said. "But I haven't eaten for two days."

"Two days?"

"My boat was wrecked on the shore and I've been looking for shelter and food until I can find a way back to England," he explained.

"England?"

"I'm from England. I was fishing. The first of the winter storms blew me too close to the Viking shores. If they find me, they'll make me a slave for sure. But if I can steal a sailing boat, I should be able to get back home."

"Will you take me with you?" Fleece asked.

She saw the man's mouth spread in a smile. "Yes, if I live long enough. But I may starve first."

The girl reached into her pocket and

pulled out the rib bone. She held it out to the stranger. "Here – take this."

The man took it. "You've saved my life," he said.

Fleece stretched out an arm and pointed down to the village below. "See the large hall in the middle?" she asked. "Meet me there after sunset. I'll show you where the Vikings keep their boats. I'll help you."

The man chewed hungrily on the bone. "Thank you, my child. Until sunset."

CHAPTER FOUR
ACCIDENT

Fleece ran down the hill. Her sledge of logs was heavy, but her feet were light. To escape to England – that was the dream that came to warm her coldest nights. Now it was so close.

As she crossed the bridge over the stream, she noticed the handrail had been smashed. She leaned over and looked down. A large man was lying in the water, face down. From the huge sword at his side, the girl knew it was Askold.

Fleece dropped the rope from the sledge and jumped into the shallow stream. She gripped the man by the shoulders and tried to lift him, but he was heavy with water. She tried to roll him, and then she tried to lift his head clear of the stream, but it was up to her knees and just too deep.

Fleece struggled through the icy water and back onto the bank. She raced over the paths, jumping over a stray pig and tripping over chickens.

The hall was dark with all the shutters closed and the torches long burned out.

"Help!" she called. "It's Askold. He has fallen in the stream. Help! He'll drown!"

Slowly, the sleeping Vikings stirred. Grumbling men rose on their shaky legs and wandered towards the door. They rubbed their eyes and blinked in the light from the lemon-grey morning sky.

Fleece tugged at sleeves and pushed legs to get the men moving towards the bridge. At last they reached the stream and stirred themselves into action.

It took four men to drag the warrior chief out of the water and throw him on his back. The pale eyes stared at the sky, as lifeless as the grey stones on the bed of the stream.

The men shook their heads. "Dead," one muttered. "He must have staggered out in the night and fallen."

"Drunk," another nodded.

"Poor Askold," a warrior sighed.

"It's better to die in battle," another agreed. "At least if he dies in battle, he goes straight to the afterlife. He feasts and fights forever more. What happens to a man who dies like this, drunk in a stream?"

"He goes to the icy halls of Hel, I guess."

The men dragged their dead leader back to the hall. Weary Vikings were spilling out onto the muddy square of earth outside. They looked grim and miserable.

"It looks like Hel for him," they all agreed.

"No!" a voice cried from the doorway.

The warriors turned and looked at the poet, who was standing there, wild-eyed and grinning.

"No," he repeated. "There *is* a way to send Askold to a better place. I was in the country of Rus and I saw the way they buried their leader. Come inside, light some torches, and I will tell you."

CHAPTER FIVE
SACRIFICE

The villagers gathered at the door of the hall. They stood in a circle around the grey-haired poet.

"In the land of Rus," he began, "they have a special Viking funeral for their chief. They make sure he goes to the Viking heaven, Valhalla."

"That's where the great god Odin lives," a woman said. "The god of war and magic."

"And every day the Viking warriors fight the trolls, the serpents and the giants," a farmer nodded.

"A wonderful life," the woman agreed.

"Each warrior has a maiden to carry his weapons. If he dies in battle, he comes back to life the next morning. It's a lovely place."

"Ah, but our chief Askold isn't going there. He died in a stream."

"He did," the woman sighed.

"Shut up," the poet said suddenly. "I am trying to tell you about the Vikings of Rus."

"Ooooh, sorry," the woman muttered.

"The Vikings there place their chief in a boat. They fill it with his weapons, so he can fight in Valhalla," the poet explained.

"Can't Odin give him some weapons when he gets there?" the farmer asked. "Odin must have lots of weapons."

The poet glared at the farmer. "Every warrior likes to fight with his own weapons. Now, as I was saying... they fill the ship with food and wine for the journey to Valhalla, and then they stuff the ship with straw."

"That'll be to feed his horse in Valhalla?" the woman asked.

"No," the poet sighed. "It is because straw burns well. They tow the boat out to sea, set it on fire and the chief's spirit is free to go to Valhalla."

"Sounds like the waste of a good ship," a fisherman grumbled.

"There's an old boat on the shore," the woman said. "It won't last the winter. We could use that. I mean, Askold has brought us a lot of food and treasure and slaves. We owe him a boat."

The villagers nodded.

"Let's get it loaded then," the farmer said.

"Wait!" the poet cried. "The chief has to have his own maiden to carry his weapons."

"I thought you said there were maidens in Valhalla," the woman reminded him.

"For the warriors who died in battle... If we're going to sneak Askold into Valhalla, we need to send him with a maiden. That's what they did in Rus. There was a slave girl on the ship when they set fire to it."

"Dad!" Sigurd cried. "We can give our slave girl, Fleece, can't we?"

"I suppose so," his father agreed.

The villagers muttered and decided this was a good idea.

"We load Askold and his weapons into the boat, we fill it with food, tow it out and set fire to it," the farmer said.

"That's right. So where is the girl?"

The villagers looked at Sigurd. He shrugged. "She was standing next to me a few moments ago," he said. "She's gone!"

CHAPTER SIX
FLIGHT

Fleece didn't know where she was going. She heard the Viking plan and ran. Over the bridge and the stream, across the dew-damp fields and up the path to the trees.

The English man in the hat was gone. She had to stay away from the village until sunset. Then she could slip back in the dark, meet the stranger and escape with him.

There was nowhere to hide in the little wood. The leaves were falling and the trees were almost bare. It was too cold to hide on the hillside, and if they set out to search they would see her.

"The shelter," she said. "I can stay in the stone sheep shelter until dark."

Fleece set off through the trees. If she ran over the hill, they would see her from the village. She headed to the valley beyond the hill. It would take her half the morning, but that didn't matter. That way she could get to the shelter without being seen.

As the sun rose higher in the sky, it gave a little warmth. She reached the sheltered side of the hill. It was just a few hundred paces to the shelter now.

Her sheep gathered around, waiting for the girl to lead them to a new grazing spot.

"Go away," she said. They started bleating and trotting around her. Over the noise, she heard voices shouting.

"She must be over there with the sheep. Go and look!"

Fleece took off her jacket and turned it inside out so the wool was on the outside.

Then she threw herself down on her hands and knees in the middle of the flock. She peered over the backs of the sheep and saw a warrior looking down at the flock.

"No," he cried over his shoulder. "She's not here!"

Another villager shouted, "There's someone in the trees where she gathers firewood! Maybe that's her..."

The warrior ran off and the voices faded. Fleece stood up and ran to the top of the hill. She saw the backs of the running hunters. The shelter was ten paces to her left.

She hurried across to it. It was a small stone hut. She had covered it in earth to keep out the draughts and it was dark inside.

The doorway was small and low, just big enough for her. She slipped into the warm safety and sighed. The hunters must have looked in here when they were on the hill. They wouldn't search the same spot again.

"Safe," she breathed.

"Good morning, slave girl," Sigurd said from the darkness. "I thought you might come here," he sniggered. "Well, I've caught you now. I'll be a hero in the village." The boy grabbed her roughly and pushed her back through the door. "Come along, slave girl. Time to go to Valhalla."

CHAPTER SEVEN
THE BOAT

Sigurd pushed Fleece down the hill ahead of him. The hunters saw him and came towards them. There was no chance of escape now.

"Ha!" the boy cried. "It's funny, isn't it? I'm going to send you to your death just like *my* father sent *your* father to his death."

"What?" Fleece said, and stopped.

The boy brought his face close to hers. "You didn't know that, did you, slave girl? My father used to be one of Askold's warriors. He raided England and attacked a farm. When your father tried to stop our warriors, my father struck him in the eye with his sword. Then he took his child for a slave. That was you. That's why you're *our* slave. You didn't know, did you?"

"So my father is dead?"

"Probably," Sigurd shrugged.

Fleece nodded, and then trudged on to the village where the Vikings were waiting for her. The villagers cheered the smirking Sigurd and slapped him on the back.

"The boat is ready," the poet said. "We're just waiting for the girl. Bring her to the shore." He led the way.

But, when they reached the sandy beach and the battered boat, they saw a man with a staff was waiting there. He wore a wide-brimmed hat and a blue cloak.

"Who's that?" a woman asked. "It looks like Odin himself."

Fleece knew it was the English stranger. Now they would kill him, too.

"Greetings," the man said.

"Who are you?" the woman asked.

"You just told your friends – I am Odin himself," the man replied.

"Odin? With the voice of an Englishman?" a warrior jeered.

"Yes, Odin has just one eye!" the woman went on.

The stranger raised a hand and lifted his hat. The villagers and warriors took a step back in surprise. 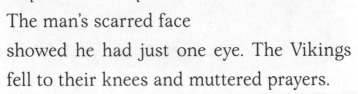 The man's scarred face showed he had just one eye. The Vikings fell to their knees and muttered prayers.

"Enough!" the stranger said. "I am Odin and I've come to take your chief to Valhalla myself. Push the boat out, and I will sail it over the oceans to the end of the world."

"What about the slave girl?" Sigurd asked.

"She can come as my servant. I'll take care of her. Lift her onto the boat."

The Vikings hurried to obey, and the strongest of the warriors pushed the boat into the water.

The one-eyed man raised the sail and let the cold, easterly wind push them away from the shore. The Vikings watched, dumb, as the boat drifted over the horizon.

"I never thought I'd meet the great god Odin," the poet said. "I must go and write a poem about it."

"It is a great day for the village," Sigurd said.

"It is," his father agreed. "But... but I am sure I have seen that man before."

"Where, Father?"

"I don't know... perhaps in a dream, eh? It doesn't matter. Let's go home. Without a slave girl, you'll have to do more work on the farm."

"What?" Sigurd wailed. "I'm not working like a slave. I won't. I refuse."

"Then I'll beat you until you do," his father promised. "Come along."

CHAPTER EIGHT
HOME

"You're not really Odin, are you?"
Fleece said.

"No, I am just
a shipwrecked
Englishman. But I saw
what was happening
and I had to do
something."

"You risked your
life," the girl said.

The man shrugged.
"We can't let the Vikings
scare us. We have to stand against them."

The grey waters slapped the rotten hull as the ship ploughed through the waves.

"It will last until we get to England," the man said. "And Askold's food will feed us on the journey. I live by Jarrow on the River Tyne. It's about a day's sailing away. We can give Askold a proper burial at the monastery there."

"What will happen to me?" Fleece asked. "Will I be *your* slave now?"

"No, no!" the man laughed. "You can be one of my family. I once had a daughter your age."

"What happened to her?"

"She was captured by Viking raiders. Oh, I tried to stop them, but I was only carrying a wooden crook for the sheep. One of their warriors attacked me with a sword. I had no chance. He struck me in the eye. They thought I was dead. I recovered... but my daughter was gone.

"My wife says they threw her into a ship before they left. Every summer since, I have sailed to Norway... I trade with the Vikings. But really I am looking for Hilda."

"Is that my name?" Fleece said quietly.

The man turned his one eye slowly towards the girl. "Hilda?"

"I was stolen from England by my master in the village," Fleece explained.

"The Vikings stole many children," the man said.

"This morning, the farmer's son told me that my master killed my father... struck him in the eye and left him for dead."

The man gazed at her. His one eye filled with a tear. He clutched the girl to him. "Your mother will think it's a miracle."

"Perhaps it is," Hilda said.

The two stood at the front of the ship and saw a dark smudge that was land ahead. Seagulls screeched over their heads as if to welcome them.

The man hugged his daughter closer. "We're going home, Hilda. We're going home."

EPILOGUE

No one knows why the Vikings left their farms and turned into raiders in around 750 CE. Maybe the farms were too poor to feed them. Maybe they needed slaves to grow enough food. Maybe stealing from monks and farmers was an easier life. Or maybe they just enjoyed the adventure of sailing the seas and fighting.

The Vikings loved to hear tales of Odin and the gods. They really believed that men who died in battle would have a better afterlife. Their greatest chiefs and warriors were buried with their weapons and some were even buried in their ships.

There was one place in the Viking world, though, that was really cruel. The land of Rus is the place we now call Russia. In Rus, they had a savage custom: they would sacrifice a slave girl so their chief would have a servant in Valhalla. The story of Fleece is not true – but some poor girls really did suffer this horrible death.

The Vikings were great sailors and some were brave warriors. They fought hard to feed their families. But they could also be the cruellest people in a cruel world.

YOU TRY

1. The great escape

Imagine you are trapped in a classroom with a truly terrible teacher. You agree with a friend that you need to escape. You may get out of the classroom – but, like Fleece crossing the hills, you mustn't be seen leaving the school.

Draw a plan of your school, and mark your escape route. Then come up with a plan to distract the child-catchers, so you have time to get home and lock the door before they come looking for you.

2. Wanted

Imagine you are a Viking slave, and that you've run away. Your masters want you back because you are worth a lot of money.

Design the 'Wanted' poster they would create for traders to carry around from village to village. It should include a picture of you, describe three important things about you, and offer a gold piece if you are brought back to your owner.

Terry Deary
Saxon Tales

The King who Throw Away his Throne

The Shepherd who Ate his Sheep

The Witch who Faced the Fire

The Lord who Lost his Head

Find more fantastically fun (and sometimes gory)
adventures in Terry Deary's Saxon Tales.
Based on real historical events!